Dear Parent:

Congratulations! Your child is taking the first steps on an exciting journey. The destination? Independent reading!

D0485425

STEP INTO READING® will help your child get there. The program offers five steps to reading success. Each step includes fun stories and colorful art. There are also Step into Reading Sticker Books, Step into Reading Math Readers, Step into Reading Phonics Readers, Step into Reading Write-In Readers, and Step into Reading Phonics Boxed Sets—a complete literacy program with something to interest every child.

Learning to Read, Step by Step!

Ready to Read   Preschool–Kindergarten
• big type and easy words • rhyme and rhythm • picture clues
For children who know the alphabet and are eager to begin reading.

Reading with Help   Preschool–Grade 1
• basic vocabulary • short sentences • simple stories
For children who recognize familiar words and sound out new words with help.

Reading on Your Own   Grades 1–3
• engaging characters • easy-to-follow plots • popular topics
For children who are ready to read on their own.

Reading Paragraphs   Grades 2–3
• challenging vocabulary • short paragraphs • exciting stories
For newly independent readers who read simple sentences with confidence.

Ready for Chapters   Grades 2–4
• chapters • longer paragraphs • full-color art
For children who want to take the plunge into chapter books but still like colorful pictures.

STEP INTO READING® is designed to give every child a successful reading experience. The grade levels are only guides. Children can progress through the steps at their own speed, developing confidence in their reading, no matter what their grade.

Remember, a lifetime love of reading starts with a single step!

Read Around
Sesame Street

Visit us on the Web!
StepIntoReading.com
SesameStreetBooks.com
randomhouse.com/kids

Educators and librarians, for a variety of teaching tools, visit us at RHTeachersLibrarians.com

ISBN: 978-0-385-37411-8

MANUFACTURED IN CHINA
10 9 8 7 6 5 4 3 2 1

STEP INTO READING®

Read Around Sesame Street

Step 1 and 2 Books

A Collection of Five Early Readers

Random House 🏠 New York

Contents

SESAME STREET

B Is for Books!

by Annie Cobb
illustrated by Joe Mathieu

B is for books.

All kinds of books.

Books about counting.

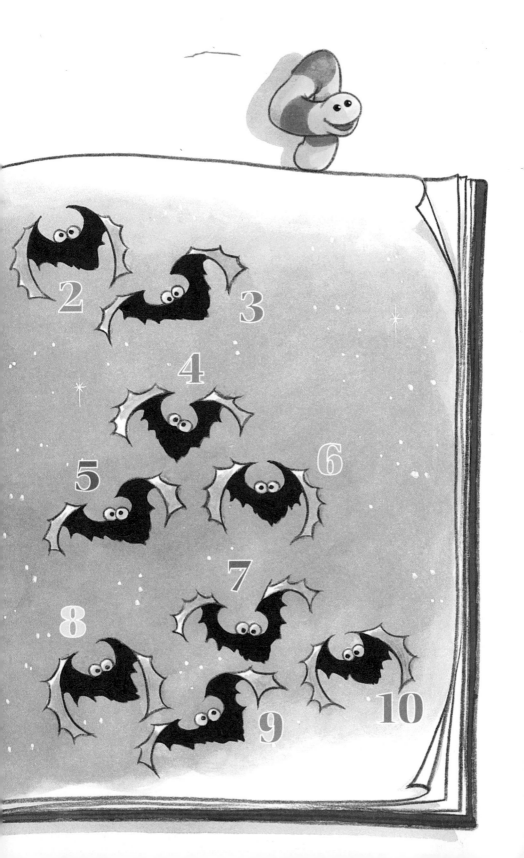

Books about cooks.

Books about blue things.

Books about birds.

Books about true things.

Books about words.

wrap

wagon

whale

worm

Books about bodies.

hair · head · hand · ear · elbow · arm · belly button · leg · foot · head · body

Books about beads.

Books about magic.

Books about weeds.

Books full of poems.

Rain, rain, go away.

Come again another day.

Books full of maps.

Books good for playtime.

Books good for naps.

Rock-a-bye baby, on the treetop.

Books full of stories.

Books full of stars.

Books full of riddles.

Books full of cars.

Books about letters

from A to Z.

Once upon
a time…

36

B is for books.

And books are for me!

I Can Do It!

SESAME STREET

by Sarah Albee

illustrated by Larry DiFiori

I can write my name.

I can draw a smile.

We can rake the leaves,
then jump into the pile.

I can slide down a slide.

I can make a cat from clay.

I can eat a lima bean.

I can dance ballet.

I don't know how
to tie my shoe.
With the help of a friend
I can learn that, too!

I can bang on a drum.

I can reach a high shelf.

I can comb my fur.

I can pour my juice myself.

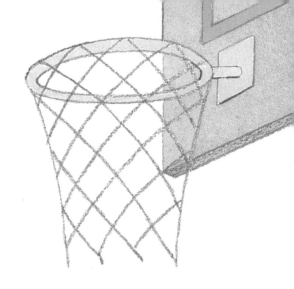

I'm too small
to dunk the ball.

I need help from my friend
who is eight feet tall.

I can button my shirt.

I can string some beads.

We can jump so high.

We can plant some seeds.

I'm too little
for a two-wheel bike.
My friend is too big
to fit on my trike!

I can't read this book.

You can't climb this tree.

I can help you up.

You can read to me!

I can carry the cups.

I can carry the plates.

Please do not try this
on roller skates!

I can watch a parade,
but little Natasha can't see!
She needs help from . . .

... a big monster like me!

SESAME STREET

Elmo Says ACHOO!

by Sarah Albee
illustrated by Tom Brannon

Elmo has a present!

What is it?

No one knows.

He is taking it
to Oscar.

It tickles Elmo's nose.

"Achoo!" Elmo sneezes.
Down blow
all the clothes!

Bert is stacking cans.
He stacks them
neat and tall.

"Achoo!" Elmo sneezes.

All the soup cans fall.

Elmo sees a person
in the barber's chair.

"Achoo!" Elmo sneezes.
Down falls all the hair!

"Look at what we built!"

the happy monsters call.

"Achoo!" Elmo sneezes.

Down falls the wall!

Here comes a parade!
The circus is in town.

"Achoo!" Elmo sneezes.
The clowns
all tumble down.

Elmo visits Oscar
to give the grouch
his gift.

"A stinkweed plant!"
says Oscar.
"The best
I ever sniffed!"

Oscar finds his hanky.

Then what does he do?

Oscar grins a grouchy grin.
And then he says . . .

SESAME STREET

Monsters Munch Lunch!

by Abigail Tabby

illustrated by Louis Womble

Tummies rumble.

Monsters grumble.

Monsters want lunch!

It is lunchtime!

Stopping.

Shopping.

Dropping.

Mopping.

Tummies rumble.

Monsters grumble.

Monsters want lunch!

Whip. Flip.

Sip. Drip.

Tummies rumble.

Monsters grumble.

Monsters want lunch!

Make shake.

Bake cake.

Tummies rumble.

Monsters grumble.

Monsters want lunch!

Slice. Dice.

Ice. Nice!

Tummies rumble.

Monsters grumble.

Monsters want lunch!

Whisk. Brisk.

Tsk tsk! . . .

Tummies rumble.

Monsters grumble.

Monsters want lunch!

Stick. Lick.

Flick. Ick!

Tummies rumble.

Monsters grumble.

Monsters want lunch!

Fry. Cry.

Why? Dry.

Tummies rumble.

Monsters grumble.

Monsters want lunch!

Tummies rumble.

Monsters grumble.

Monsters want lunch

. . . NOW!

Please.

Munch! Crunch!
Yum! Lunch!

Monsters munch lunch!
Yum!

Cookie Monster is ready for dinner!

Baker, Baker, Cookie Maker

SESAME STREET

by Linda Hayward

illustrated by Tom Brannon

Cookie Monster,
cookie eater,
mixes batter
with his beater,

130

drops the dough
onto the sheet,

bakes the cookies.

Good to eat!

He puts the cookies
on a plate,
takes a cookie . . .
Oops, too late!

135

Baker, baker,
cookie maker,
here comes a hungry
cookie taker!

COOKIES! COOKIES!

Monster treat.

Some for munchers,
some for crunchers,

none for the baker

on Sesame Street.

Cookie Monster,

cookie cutter,

makes a batch

with peanut butter,

cuts the cookies
out of dough,

puts them on the plate . . .

Oh, no!

Baker, baker,
cookie maker,
here comes another
cookie taker!

COOKIES! COOKIES!

Monster treat.

Some for hikers,
some for bikers,

none for the baker

on Sesame Street.

Cookie Monster,
cookie master,
makes more cookies
even faster.

He pats the cookies
nice and flat;
makes them,
bakes them.
Look at that!

Baker, baker,
cookie maker,
here come some *more*
cookie takers!

COOKIES! COOKIES!

Monster treat.

Some for hoppers,
some for moppers,

and *one* for the baker
on Sesame Street.